D1309548

 **A GOLDEN BOOK • NEW YORK**

Special thanks to Sarah Buzby, Cindy Ledermann, Vicki Jaeger, Dana Koplik, Ann McNeill, Emily Kelly, Sharon Woloszyk, Julia Phelps, Tanya Mann, Rob Hudnut, David Wiebe, Tiffany J. Shuttleworth, Gabrielle Miles, Rainmaker Entertainment, Walter P. Martishius, Carla Alford, Rita Lichtwardt, and Kathy Berry

BARBIE and associated trademarks and trade dress are owned by, and used under license from, Mattel, Inc. Copyright © 2012 Mattel, Inc. All Rights Reserved.
Published in the United States by Golden Books, an imprint of Random House Children's Books, a division of Random House, Inc., 1745 Broadway, New York, NY 10019, and in Canada by Random House of Canada Limited, Toronto. No part of this book may be reproduced or copied in any form without permission from the copyright owner. Golden Books, A Golden Book, A Big Golden Book, the G colophon, and the distinctive gold spine are registered trademarks of Random House, Inc.

www.barbie.com
randomhouse.com/kids
ISBN: 978-0-307-93036-1
Printed in the United States of America
10 9 8 7 6 5 4 3 2

Adapted by Kristen L. Depken
Based on the original screenplay by Elise Allen
Illustrated by Ulkutay Design Group

It was a sunny afternoon in Malibu. Merliah Summers was surfing in a competition against her biggest rival, Kylie Morgan, who was from Australia.

Merliah and Kylie caught the same wave and crisscrossed each other's paths, showing off their best tricks. Merliah finished her run with an impressive flip, then caught a wave to shore.

Soon an announcer declared Merliah the winner, with Kylie in second place. That meant both girls would go to Australia to surf in the World Championship Surf Invitational.

"You were lucky, mate," Kylie sneered. "But your luck's gonna run out down under—that's *my* turf."

Excited to share her news, Merliah gripped her seashell necklace and said, "I wish to become a mermaid." Suddenly, a swirl of magic turned her legs into a shimmering tail. Merliah had a special secret—she was a mermaid princess! Her mother, Calissa, was the queen of the undersea kingdom of Oceana.

Merliah dove into the ocean with her baby sea lion friend, Snouts. Calissa and her pink dolphin companion, Zuma, congratulated Merliah when she told them about her win.

Calissa had some important news to share, too. It was almost time for the Changing of the Tides ceremony.

"Every twenty years," the queen explained, "a member of the royal family must return to the underwater city of Aquellia, sit atop the ancient throne, and regain the power to make Merillia, the magical life force of the ocean." Performing the ceremony revealed a mermaid's truest self.

"I believe that if you were to perform the ceremony, you'd become a mermaid and lose the power to become human," Calissa told Merliah. "I'd never ask you to do it. I just hope you'll be there to watch."

Unfortunately, the ceremony was on the same day as the surfing
competition in Australia.

"You are the princess of Oceana," Calissa told her daughter.
"You must be at the ceremony."

But the world championship was too important to Merliah.
"I can't make it," she said, and swam off in a hurry.

Two weeks later, Merliah and Kylie arrived in Australia for the first heat of the competition. Both surfers had awesome runs, but this time Kylie took first place and Merliah came in second.

"I stomped all over you!" gloated Kylie.

However, a handstand that Merliah had performed during the competition drew the attention of reporters, photographers, and fans—including Georgie Majors, the head of Wavecrest Surf Gear. Georgie asked Merliah to star in Wavecrest's new ad campaign! "But *I* won the heat!" Kylie cried in frustration.

During a luau that evening, Kylie sat sulking on a dock. She was startled when a rainbow fish popped out of the water—and began talking to her!

"I can tell you how to beat Merliah Summers tomorrow," said the fish, whose name was Alistair. "She has a necklace that gives her special powers. You take the necklace, you take her powers."

While Merliah was busy at a photo shoot for Wavecrest, Kylie secretly stole her seashell necklace from the pocket of her sweatshirt.

When Kylie got back to the dock, Alistair
told her to put the necklace on and wish to
become a mermaid. Kylie obeyed, and her legs
magically transformed into a beautiful tail.
"Now follow me!" commanded the fish.
Curious, Kylie dove into the ocean and
discovered that she could breathe underwater!

Soon Kylie and Alistair arrived at a huge whirlpool.
"Your Majesty, I've brought you the girl," said Alistair.
Before Kylie knew what was happening, the fish had pushed her
over the edge!
As Kylie was sucked into the whirlpool, a mermaid shot out. It was
Merliah's evil aunt Eris! A year before, Eris had tried to take over
Oceana, but Merliah had trapped her in the whirlpool. Eris had been
determined to escape and take her revenge ever since.

"Well done, Alistair," Eris said once she was free. "Now we have to make sure I'm on the throne of Aquellia for the ceremony. Then I'll have the power to make Merillia, and the ocean will be mine!" As Eris and Alistair swam off, Kylie cried for help.

Luckily, Snouts had followed Kylie and Alistair. He heard Kylie's cries and hurried back to the beach, where Merliah and her friends were frantically looking for her missing necklace.

"Snouts, are you saying Kylie has something to do with my necklace?" asked Merliah. The sea lion barked excitedly, and Merliah followed him into the ocean. She couldn't change into a mermaid without her necklace, but she could still breathe underwater.

When Merliah and Snouts reached the whirlpool, they heard
Kylie calling for help. Merliah quickly made a rope from seaweed.
She tied one end to a nearby rock and fastened the other around
her ankle, then dove into the whirlpool.

The whirlpool spit Kylie out—and sucked Merliah in!
Kylie grabbed the end of the seaweed rope just in time.
"I've got you!" yelled Kylie. She and Snouts worked
together to pull Merliah out.

"I never should have taken your necklace," Kylie told Merliah when they were both safe. Kylie needed to keep the necklace to breathe underwater, but she promised to give it back on land.

Merliah explained that she had to stop Eris. "If my aunt is free, she will find a way to control the ocean and enslave every living thing in it," she said.

"Then I'm going with you," said Kylie.

Meanwhile, in nearby Aquellia, Calissa was welcoming ambassadors from other parts of the ocean. They had each brought a jewel that would be an important part of the Changing of the Tides ceremony. At noon, a shaft of sunlight would shine down, bouncing from one jewel to the next until it landed on the throne, granting whoever was sitting there the power to make Merillia.

As they were preparing for the ceremony, the ambassadors heard a chilling voice. "What, you're not setting a place for me?"

"Eris!" Calissa cried.

Eris was followed by Alistair and an army of tough electric fish called stargazers. The stargazers captured the ambassadors while Eris went after Calissa.

Using a spell that made her enemy's worst nightmare come true, Eris turned Calissa's tail to stone.

"No!" cried Calissa as she sank to the bottom of the ocean, unable to swim.

Eris cast the nightmare spell on the rest of the ambassadors and locked them in a cage, then prepared to take the throne.

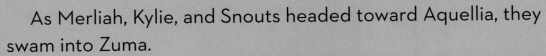

As Merliah, Kylie, and Snouts headed toward Aquellia, they swam into Zuma.

"Merliah, your mother!" cried Zuma. "She's in terrible danger!"

Merliah and her friends quickly followed Zuma to the spot where Calissa was trapped. They tried to pull the queen from the ocean floor, but her stone tail was too heavy.

"The only way Eris will be stopped is if another member of the royal family performs the ceremony," said Merliah.

"Merliah," warned Calissa, "if you do it, you'll lose your legs—forever."

"I know," said Merliah. "But I'm the princess of Oceana. It's my duty."

Kylie, Snouts, and Zuma vowed to help Merliah. They quickly came up with a plan.

The friends snuck into the ceremony and tied up all but two of Eris's stargazers. Merliah and Kylie jumped onto them and rode them like surfboards—right toward Eris.

"Merliah!" Eris shouted angrily.

The girls used their surfing skills to keep Eris busy while
Zuma and Snouts freed the ambassadors.
Suddenly, a shaft of sunlight reflected off the first gem.
The ceremony was beginning!
Kylie steered her stargazer close enough to give Eris
a shock, knocking her off the throne.

Merliah quickly sat on the throne, but Eris soon recovered and began hurling bolts of magic at her. Zuma, Snouts, and the ambassadors threw rocks and pieces of coral at the evil mermaid.

Then Eris changed direction and aimed a blast of magic at one
of the gems, shattering it.

"What have you done?" cried Merliah.

Just as the ray of sunlight was about to hit the shattered gem,
Kylie zoomed over and put a shiny seashell in its place.

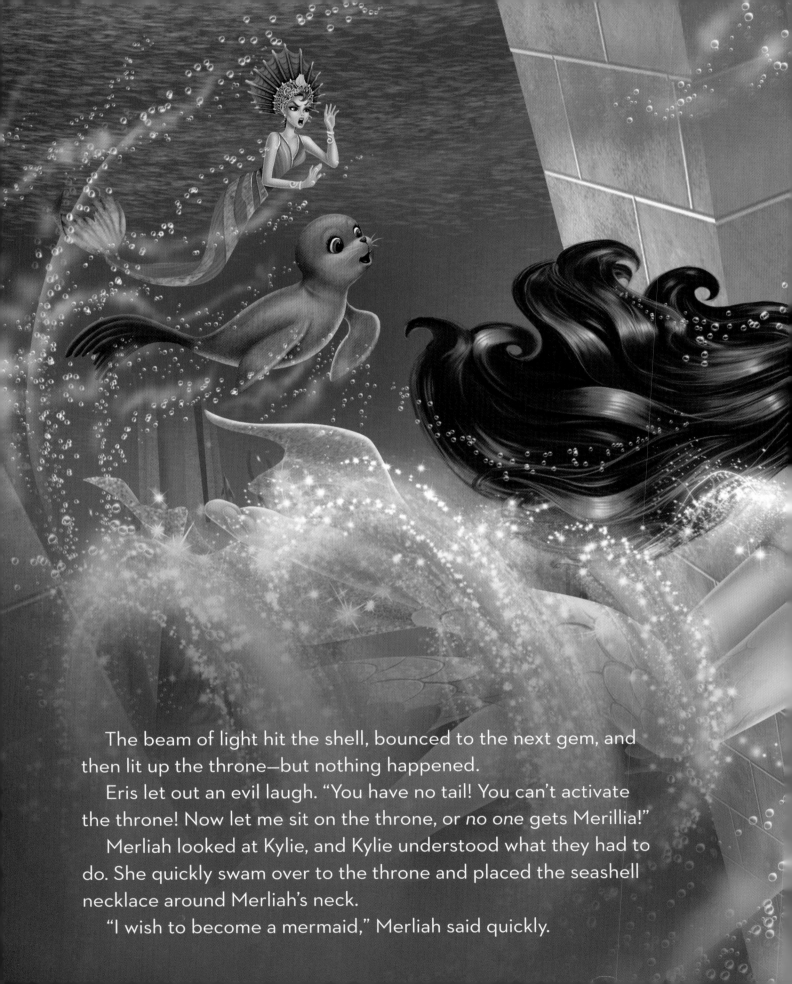

The beam of light hit the shell, bounced to the next gem, and then lit up the throne—but nothing happened.

Eris let out an evil laugh. "You have no tail! You can't activate the throne! Now let me sit on the throne, or *no one* gets Merillia!"

Merliah looked at Kylie, and Kylie understood what they had to do. She quickly swam over to the throne and placed the seashell necklace around Merliah's neck.

"I wish to become a mermaid," Merliah said quickly.

Merliah's tail spread across the throne, activating its magic. Soon Merliah was surrounded by a bubble of shimmering lights and glowing colors. Her hair and tail began to grow longer and more brilliant. Everyone looked on in amazement.

"Noooo!" cried Eris. She shot a bolt of magic at the throne—but it shot right back at her. She fell into a bed of kelp, unconscious, and all the nightmare spells she had cast came undone.

When the magic began to fade, Merliah rushed over and slipped the seashell necklace around her friend's neck.

"I wish to become a mermaid," Kylie murmured with her last bit of breath. Gasping for air, she turned back into a mermaid. "How did we do?"

Merliah smiled with relief. "It was a perfect ten."

Calissa swam over to Merliah and Kylie, her tail back to normal. "I'm so proud of you. Both of you," she said.

Then Eris awoke and screamed. She had cast the spell on herself. Her worst nightmare had come true. Her magic was gone—and she had legs!

"No!" she cried as the ambassadors took her away.

Calissa encouraged Merliah to try out her new power to make Merillia. "You'll find you can make Merillia doing anything you love," she explained.

Looking down at her tail, Merliah realized that she would no longer be able to surf in the championship.

"That means it's even more important for *you* to go out there and surf," Merliah told Kylie. "For both of us."

Together, Merliah, Kylie, and Calissa swam to the surface.

The final heat of the world championship was about to begin. Kylie wished to be a human again. When her legs returned, she handed the necklace back to Merliah.

But Calissa insisted that she keep it. "The necklace is yours now. We need another ambassador—someone who experiences the ocean from above. Will you help us?"

"I would be honored," said Kylie.

Merliah sighed. "I had a sweet new trick planned for today's run," she said to Calissa. "I wish I could still surf so I could show it to Kylie." Suddenly, a swirl of magic turned Merliah's tail into legs!

"The ceremony did transform you into your truest self, but I can see now that your truest self is both a mermaid *and* a human!" explained Calissa. "You don't need a necklace to help you change."

"You can surf in the meet!" Kylie cried. "Come on!"

The girls grabbed their boards just as a big, beautiful wave approached.

"May the best surfer win!" said Merliah. She and Kylie both dropped into the wave and began doing trick after trick. The crowd on the beach went wild.

Merliah slowed down and stared in awe at a shimmering trail behind her.

"I'm making Merillia!" she cried. "This is better than the contest!"

"Then I'm going to slam it home!" replied Kylie.

Merliah smiled as she watched Kylie pull off her best move yet.

Back on shore, Kylie was immediately surrounded by photographers and fans.

"First place in the World Championship Surf Invitational: Kylie Morgan!" Kylie stepped forward to accept her trophy, pulling Merliah up with her.

"This is *your* moment!" protested Merliah.

Kylie smiled. "I never could have done this without you," she said.

Together, the girls raised the trophy in the air to celebrate their victory—and their new friendship.

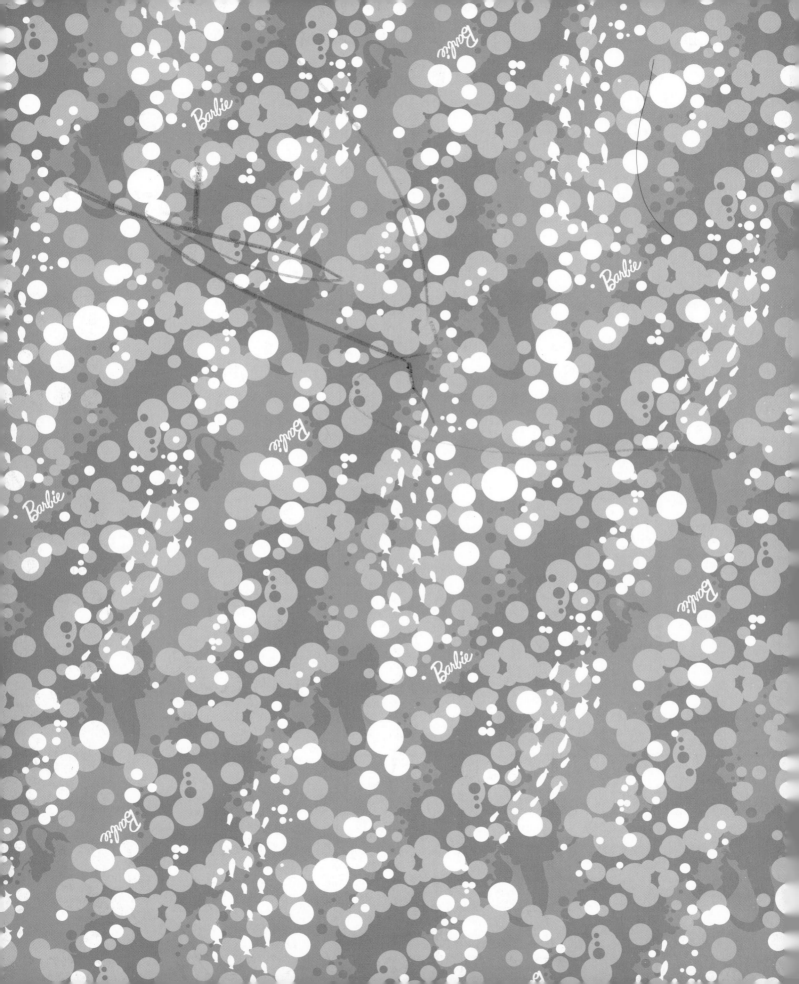